Very Fine People

D1518330

Written by Henry Charles

Edited by Michelle Bodden-White

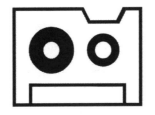

Hiztory Bookz • New York
Read. Educate.

ISBN: 9798652421052
ISBN-13:

DEDICATION

This book is dedicated to Marie-Solange and Henry Charles; my beloved parents, who migrated from the beautiful country of Haiti, enroute for the American dream. Thank you. I love you both. I will see you again.

To my wife Melanie Gould and my son Henry, III.
Thank you for always believing in me.

To the entire Austin family tree!
(My siblings Carine, Andre and Marie-Carmelle)
Thank you for always having my back, through thick and thin.

To everyone in Far Rockaway!

To my Jackson State University family!

To the victims and all affected by the Tulsa, Oklahoma massacre in 1921;
WE WILL NEVER FORGET.

Last but not least.
WBAI Radio 99.5FM, (Pacifica Radio) thank you for shedding the light!.

CONTENTS   PAGE

Foreword

BY **HENRY CHARLES**

My inspiration behind writing this novel came when I stumbled upon listening to the wrong radio station while driving home from work. I became intrigued when I heard the voice of an elderly woman, explaining what she had witnessed as a child. Her raspy but soothing voice was touching. She vividly remembered white men breaking into her mother's home, while her mother was cooking dinner. She recalled white men looting their possessions. Surprisingly, she said her mother just continued to cook and ordered her to get under the kitchen table. She went on to explain the horrific things she saw and still remembered. When her mother finally decided to leave, she said there was fire everywhere; the city was literally on fire.

At that moment I was hooked! However, I felt helpless. I was angry, shocked, and sad. I wished I could have gone back in time and fought. When the segment ended, I wanted to know more and hear more about this senseless riot that destroyed a powerful black community, which also killed hundreds of innocent black people. Once I reached home I began doing my research on this terrible American tragedy.

My story of Mr. Maddox Dublin and his family are fiction, but the story of the Tulsa, Oklahoma race riot is real. Despite being a fictional novel. I inserted actual African-American figures who some people would never hear about. For example, "Blind Tom" Wiggins! He was regarded as the best piano player in the mid 1800s. Not to mention, he was born a slave, blind and autistic. Respectfully, before Stevie Wonder and Ray Charles, there was Blind Tom.

I hope after reading this book, I have encouraged you to research the people and businesses that made up the "Black Wall Street," and what it could have been if the riots never occurred.

Chapter One

THE DUBLINS

James is the son of Mr. Maddox Dublin, the son of a funeral home owner. Mr. Maddox Dublin is known all around town as a good man; a hard worker who knows everyone in town because of his funeral home. Mr. Dublin and his son James are the only African Americans living in a small town, right outside of Tulsa, Oklahoma. The rest of the African Americans evacuated town and were forced to leave without their possessions after the town riots which killed over 300 people, mostly African Americans. Mr. Maddox Dublin goes out of his way preparing the dead bodies of loved ones from town who passed away. He would give discounts to people's families if their loved ones died a tragic or untimely death. That is what got him a good reputation around town. In 1921, times were looking up for blacks in Tulsa, Oklahoma. The Dublin family made a good name for themselves. They were known around town for their soul-food restaurant called "Dublin Good."Maddox Dublin, a dark skinned man with a muscular build in his thirties, worked in the kitchen with his parents. He was married with a newborn baby at home. At a time in the south where racial tension was very high, people said the food at Dublin Good was so good; it would change the mind of any Ku Klux Klan member. One of the items on the menu that had people buzzing around town was the fried chicken! The fried chicken was to die for; crispy, juicy and flavorful. When it came to dessert, a slice of Maebelle's pecan pie would make a friend out of anyone. Sometimes the restaurant would be so packed; the service line would be out the door. When that happened, Mrs. Dublin would go out and serve all those waiting in line with a complimentary slice of pecan pie and ice tea or water. Mr. And Mrs Dublin understood how hard the people around town worked and how harsh the heat could be, so they did what they could to accommodate those waiting on line. The service was good and the food was Dublin good!

It was one of those hot sweltering days in Tulsa when Todd Macintosh led a group of young white boys into town in a red pick-up truck, throwing rocks and beer bottles at people, houses and businesses. They were also yelling obscenities at the blacks in town. Some of the customers began walking off the line. Afraid of getting hurt; one by one, two by two, people were scurrying off the service line which once again wrapped around the restaurant. Then Mrs. Dublin shouted out, "what am I gonna do with all this pie?"

Some of the men turned back, some were all too familiar with young Todd Macintosh. As the truck got closer and closer, concerned for her safety, one of the customers on line demanded for Mrs. Dublin to get inside the restaurant.

"Maebelle, right now is not the time for pie, go'on inside now!"

She replied, "I'm ok, I'm just fine sugar."

Mr. Dublin calmly walks into the restaurant to fetch his shotgun. The teenage boys, out of things to throw, jumped out of the pick-up truck. The black men who didn't run away were hungry and exhausted from work. However, they were ready to fight if it came down to protecting themselves and their town.

Todd Macintosh stumbled out of the driver side door, with his six friends behind him, all wearing worn-down, blue denim overalls. Todd Macintosh stands about six feet tall, with blond hair, blue eyes. He said, "We don't like you people, you monkeys!"

Behind him, his friends instigated, "yea, yea, you monkeys smell."

Todd opened his mouth and before another insult came out of it, Mrs. Dublin shoved a piece of pecan pie in it. It seemed like everything in town stopped. It got so quiet you could hear an ant run. Everyone was looking but nobody could believe what just happened and they didn't understand. Todd chewed the pie, swallowed and then he grimaced.

"Can I have some more ma'am?" said Todd.

"Suuuure, honey," replied Mrs. Dublin, she handed him the rest of the pie which was a little more than half. Mrs. Dublin grabbed Todd's arm, wiped the dirt off of his left cheek and forehead and said, "make sure you bring back my plate and tell your dad to bring back my bowls ya'hear!"

Todd nodded, jumped back into his red pick-up and sped off. Just like that, Mrs. Dublin knew how to deescalate a bad situation before it happened. This is what made the Dublin family so special around town among blacks *and whites*.

Chapter Two

FOOD FOR THE SOUL
I

Nineteen years later, Maddox Dublin now runs his own business like his parents; not a restaurant, but a funeral home. Like his parents, Maddox Dublin is well known and liked in town. Before his parents passed away, they made a fortune, secured their money and passed on their fortune to Maddox, who is now older and wiser. At forty-nine years of age, Maddox Dublin lives with his son James. Maddox Dublin stands six feet tall and his skin resembles melted chocolate, dark and smooth. He is often praised for his pristine physical shape; his broad shoulders are like the Rocky Mountains, connecting to his trapezius muscles. Mr. Dublin runs and exercises regularly. Bald head and no facial hair, Maddox Dublin speaks with a deep but soothing voice. Mr. Dublin is a mortician; he prepares the bodies in a section of his house. The home in which he and his son James live in is huge; one of the biggest homes in town and it is right next to the funeral chapel.

After preparing a body for a funeral, Mr. Dublin usually gets into banter with James about not charging people for his services. James feels that his father continues to provide his services at little or no cost, then his father will no longer be able to make a living. Mr. Dublin is very wealthy, but his son James doesn't have a clue. They would jokingly go back and forth on this topic, but James knew his father was a hardworking man. He loved, respected and admired his father very much.

"Of all people in the world, Mrs. Richardson, that old lady hates kids with a passion!" said James.

"I don't believe that, maybe if kids will stop stealing apples from her apple tree, she'd be more welcoming to kids. Besides, Mrs. Richardson lost all the men in her family to wars; great grandfather, grandfather, father, husband and now her son, her only child. You really expect me to ask her for money?" Mr. Dublin replied.

"Yes dad." James shot back. The two started laughing.

Deeds like these are what gave Mr. Dublin a good name around town, living up to his parent's reputation. No one could ever say anything negative about Mr. Dublin, except for his son James. James was known around town for two things, being his father's son and playing high school football. James' complexion matched his father's as well as his physical stature. James is the local football star. He plays tailback and has most of the high school's records. James is very popular at his high school. He has won many outstanding academic awards, along with being hailed as athletic player of the year two years in a row. There's nothing special about James, other than he likes to study and get good grades. He's just another kid. However, what makes him stand out from the other kids at his school is that he is the only black student. Sometimes he gets teased, picked on and called racial slurs because he is the only black person in school. James never loses his cool. When James is alone, he remembers what his father once told him, *"If people know what gets you angry, you will be fighting all your life."*

When James is not alone he is usually with his girlfriend, Heather Bates. Heather is white, athletic, tall, with dirty blonde hair. She is a junior in high school. She is a cheer leader with a feisty attitude and is the daughter of the town's sheriff. She is very popular throughout school and sometimes gets teased about having James as her boyfriend. However, unlike James it is difficult for Heather to ignore the negativity that surrounds her.

One day while going to retrieve a headband she had forgotten, Heather noticed there were a crowd of girls near her locker. As she got closer, she realized the crowd was in front of *her* locker. When Cindy saw Heather, she tapped Melissa and they were gone. It was a domino effect, girls were quickly dashing for the exit by two's and three's once they noticed it was Heather. For the girls who didn't leave, they were ready to see another epic battle; Heather Bates versus Christie Lane. Christie was so keen on finishing her message that she didn't realize the crowd size had decreased.

"Wait til' she sees this," muttered Christie, as she writes the letters "N-I-G."

But before Christie could write the next letter, Heather grabbed a handful of hair from the back of Christie's head and shoved her face into the metal locker, then pulled Christie down to the ground. Still holding on to her hair, Heather got on top of Christie who was motionless and dazed from the collision. Heather begins hurling lefts and rights to Christie's face. Christie's friends wanted no part of Heather, so they stood there watching.

Through all the commotion, Ms. Woods the gym teacher pushed through the crowd and yanked Heather off of Cindy. Both girls were expelled from school.

Heather would always find comfort in James. She never told James why she was always getting into fights. James would always assume that because Heather was pretty and the most popular girl at school; her peers were jealous of her, causing her to get teased and fight as a result. However, Heather never admitted to James the real reason for her getting into fights was because of him. The white girls at school couldn't fathom why a white girl would want to be with a black boy. But they all learned painful lessons. Heather and pretty much most of the students at school had knowledge of the riots that occurred 19 years ago, because of her father, but she also knew that James wasn't privy to what happened in the past. In a way, Heather was protecting James in more ways than one. Heather understood why there were no black people in town, except for the Dublins, she also thought it was not right and unfair what happened during the riots.

As school dismissed, Heather waited for James at their usual spot under the flagpole.

"I didn't see you at lunch." said James. Heather, quickly changing the subject said, "I know, "I know, come on let's go!"

The two held hands and began to walk. James felt the band aids on Heather's hand. He lifted Heather's hand up to take a closer look.

"What in the world happened to your hand? Tell me you didn't get into another fight." said James.

Puzzled, Heather had to come up with a lie, convincing enough that James would believe her.

"What! You expect me to let some stupid girl talk to me like she's my momma? My mother is dead." Heather snapped back.

"Okay… I…. Didn't know," James said gloomily.

"Listen, forget about my hand. Let me worry about my hands, okay? Just forget the whole thing, I'll race you home," said Heather. The two sprinted away. Heather reached the Dublin's property first.

"Is your dad home? asked Heather.

"I don't know, we'll find out," James replied.

Heather reached for the door knob; the door was unlocked. Heather turned the knob and opened the front door.

"How come your father always leaves the front door unlocked?" asked Heather. James and Heather entered the house before James could answer.

"Because I don't have anything anyone would want or deem as valuable, but if someone wanted to break into this house to steal something, then I would just give it to them; things can always be replaced," replied Mr. Dublin.

He walked over to James and Heather; kissing both kids on the forehead, while making his way to the kitchen.

"Are you kids hungry? How was school?" asked Mr. Dublin.

James mocks Heather by putting both of his fists up like a boxer and begins to shadow boxing. Heather smiles and whispers to James, "shut-up," then shouts to Mr. Dublin, "No, we're okay." James whispered, "But you missed lunch because you were too busy being Jack Johnson," then shouted, "Yes dad, We'll eat!"

James begins to shadow box again, throwing lefts, rights, hooks and uppercuts, teasing Heather.

"Great! We're having the Dublin's world famous fried chicken," said Mr. Dublin. "If you're gonna stay for dinner Heather, call your father and let him know," said Mr. Dublin.

"Yes sir," said Heather.

While Heather heads for the phone, James gives her privacy and enters the kitchen to join his father. As Heather talks to her father she begins to analyze the many photos on the wall. This is not the first time Heather has been in the Dublin household. However, this is the first time she pays attention to the many faces on the walls.

Everyone in the black picture frames was African-American. They were babies, infants, children, young, old, middle aged, families, friends, men and women. Heather just ignored her father's response.

"Okay dad, see you later," Heather said as she rushed off of the phone.

Heather gawked at the many photos as if she was in a museum. The living room was huge with high ceilings; shiny black wooden floors. The walls were pearl white. She stopped and stared at one photo with a woman who seemed to be a model. The woman had beautiful fair-skin, shiny black hair; done in curls. Her eyes glistened. The woman gently bit on her left index finger as if she was yearning for something. She had to be a model Heather thought. Heather began to mock the woman in the photo. She grabbed her long blonde hair and bunched it on top of her head while turning sideways, and put her index finger on her lips. Knowing she looked silly and could not match the elegance of the nameless women, Heather

laughed to herself and moved on to the next set of pictures which covered

the whole entire living room and dining room walls. There were colored

people at the beach wearing bikinis. Kids; dressed in fancy church clothing.

Men in suits standing in front of their cars, women seeming to be best of

friends huddled up to take pictures.

Heather came across a photo of men; looking very dapper in their

pin-striped, zoot suits, black shades over their eyes, tops hats with the

feather. One picture had people standing in front of the world famous

Cotton Club in Harlem, New York City. The photos were endless. There

were black men in police, army, navy and marine uniforms. Heather found

herself lost in a sea of black elegance. She was mesmerized by the number

of pictures and the variety of photos she had witnessed. Heather thought to

herself, if only the students at school could see how beautiful black people

are, maybe they would stop heckling her about being with James.

James sneaks up behind Heather and startles her.

"HA!" shouts James. Heather jumps in a scare.

"You frightened me, I should punch you!" said Heather as she

cocks back her balled fist.

"Ain't you had enough fighting for today?" James said, while laughing with his guards up.

"Who are all these people, you still don't know?" asked Heather.

"Some are relatives and most of them I don't know. My father doesn't talk about the people in the pictures much." replied James.

"Wow, so all of these people you don't know who they are," asked Heather.

"Well I know that these two are my grandparents. Back in the day, they owned a famous restaurant called Dublin Good; that's one thing that my father always talks about. He raves about that restaurant and how people would be lined up around the corner waiting to get my grandmother's famous fried chicken," said James.

She was gazing in amazement, as if this was her first time in the Dublin household seeing the framed photographs on the walls.

"Who helped your father put these pictures up again?" asked Heather.

"He put up all of these by himself," answered James.

Heather whispers, "So, so... he still didn't tell you about your mother or what happened to her?"

"Naaaw, he said he'll tell me when I get older, but for now he always says, James! James! study and make sure you get your education son," said James while mocking his father.

"James, can you make sure the dinner table is set," shouted Mr. Dublin from the kitchen.

"Already done pop!" answered James.

Mr. Dublin walks into the dining room holding a large round serving tray. On it, there was golden crisp fried chicken, sliced caramelized sweet potatoes, fresh greens along with thick and moist cornbread and a pitcher of sweet iced tea.

"You never had the world famous Dublin Good fried chicken, have you Heather?" said Mr.Dublin.

"No, but I am about to," said Heather with a big smile on her face.

"Someone will have to say grace," said Mr. Dublin. The three closed their eyes and bowed their heads.

"Oh Lord, please bless this food we are about to eat. Bless Mr. Dublin's big heart for inviting me into his home for dinner."

Heather opened her eyes and peered into the living room where the photos were and continued.

"Please bless all those who we know and love who are no longer with us."

Mr. Dublin had his eyes on Heather the whole time, as she was peeking into the living room. When she noticed Mr. Dublin looking at her, Heather quickly closed her eyes and bowed her head.

"Amen!" said the trio. They started eating.

"pass the chicken!"

"Pass the sweet potatoes!"

Clink – clank!

Clink – clank!

Ping!

Clink – clank!

The sounds of silverware meeting the porcelain plates fills the dining room.

"What happened to your hands Heather?" asked Mr. Dublin. Heather was at a loss for words, thinking fast. Heather quickly picks up a chicken leg and takes two huge chomps of chicken. Heather then turns her attention to Mr. Dublin and puts up her index finger, signaling to Mr. Dublin to give her a few seconds as she finishes chewing. Heather was thinking of a lie to tell. She didn't want Mr. Dublin to know that she had been in a fight.

GULP!

"We formed a pyramid, and I was the flyer; one of the bottom half girls buckled and I fell," said Heather.

"Hm. Good thing you didn't hurt anything else except for both hands," said Mr. Dublin.

At that moment Heather knew Mr. Dublin was on to her story. Heather shamefully bowed her head.

"I beat up Christie Lane for writing something stupid on my locker," Heather said bravely.

Mr. Dublin smiled. "I admire your honesty. Next time just come clean from the beginning." Heather smiled back, nodded and took another bit of the juicy, crispy, fried chicken.

"What happened after the fight, did you get in trouble?" ask Mr. Dublin.

With a month full of chicken Heather answered. "Yeah, my dad was pretty upset this time. They expelled me for a whole week."

"What did this Christie Lane write on your locker?" asked Mr. Dublin.

Too ashamed to tell, Heather stopped eating and sadly looked down at her plate, then looked up at Mr. Dublin making a slight grimace. Mr. Dublin knew it was something bad, he nodded slightly.

"You know after someone attacks you. They will be on guard, waiting for you to retaliate. They will have their guards up and ready. But you shouldn't retaliate. You should give it time. Let the bad blood die down. Let them think you have given up. Or even let them think you surrendered. Let the time go by. Plan, plot and strategize. When the time is right, you strike! You strike and you strike hard. You strike SO hard that they will never know what hit them." said Mr. Dublin as he gets up from the table, grabs his plate, walks to the kitchen and puts his plate in the sink.

Heather and James snickered and stared at each other. Mr. Dublin exits the kitchen and walks up the stairs. When James and Heather heard the bedroom door close, they busted out laughing.

"Remind me not to mess with your father," said Heather.

"You're the one punching people out," replied James.

Chapter Three

JUST LEAVE

"Dad it's getting closer to us, we have to go," said Maddox.

"Where am I going? this is my house!" replied his father, James Dublin.

"I can hear shooting and screaming." Says Maddox, while he paces back and forth to the living room, where his mother is holding her grandson James; and his father sits calmly eating dinner.

"Mom, dad, it's not safe here anymore, we have to leave." Maddox is interrupted by a disturbing bang on the front door.

Boom!-Boom!-Boom!-Boom!

Everyone is silenced by the hard banging and stares at the front door. "Maebelle. Get me my shotgun," whispered James. Maddox quickly *runs into the kitchen and grabs the biggest knife and fearlessly marches towards the front door. The person on the other side of the door decided to give it another knock. This time the knock was harder and faster.*

Boom!-Boom!-Boom!-Boom!-Boom!-Boom!-Boom!-Boom!

Maddox raised his right hand which gripped the large sharp kitchen knife; with his left hand he grabbed the doorknob. Maddox closed his eyes, inhaling deep. Held it in, counted to five; 1... 2... 3... 4... 5. Maddox exhaled through his mouth slowly. Then he opened his eyes, made a grimace and quickly opened the door.

No one was there. All you could hear was the ruckus from a half mile down into the city. Maddox poked his head out of the doorway to make sure no one was outside. Maddox cautiously pulls himself back inside of the house and begins to close the door, that's when a hand slams on the door keeping it from closing. Maddox quickly raised the kitchen knife in a striking motion. A familiar voice comes from behind the door.

"WAAAIT!" frantically said the person.

It was Mike Jones, Maddox's childhood friend. Mike stood about five feet, eight inches tall; all muscle. He is what some people in the south would call "country strong." He was tough as an ox. For fun he would

chop down huge trees, run along the train tracks and race the locomotive

trains, and when he was bored, he would go "cow tipping," then he would

get in trouble because Mrs. Florence would tell on him. The hardest thing

in the world is trying to get a cow back up on all-fours. Mike would carry a

few logs of wood at a time to build homes with his father. Usually it would

take a herd of cattle to haul the wood. Mike had no problems with manual

labor; he loved to build homes and businesses with his father. The two built

most of the new homes and business structures in town. Their company,

Black Water Construction, was always busy, even in the winter season.

Mike and his father took pride in their business because they employed

most of the people from town who didn't have a job or couldn't find any

work. Their contribution was heavily appreciated in town. Sometimes, Mike

and his father wouldn't charge for their services. If they felt their

community needed a movie theater or park, they built it with no problems.

Mike and his father were very wealthy and thought of it as investing in their

town for a better community; everyone contributed one way or the other.

"Oh my god, baby no." said Maebelle after seeing Mike. Mike's

shirt was torn from the collar and had splattered red stains, which seemed to be blood that didn't come from him. He had scratches and bruises on his face. The skin on his knuckles were scraped off. He was breathing heavily.

"Man why didn't you come to the door when I first opened it?" asked Maddox.

"I knocked on the door, no one answered, so I went round-back to see if anyone was there. I came back around and saw the shadow of your funny shaped head." replied Mike.

The two hugged each other and started laughing. But no one joined in their childhood humor.

"Mike, what's going on out there?" asked Maddox's wife Jewel.

"That's why I came here. Most of the town is clearing out, but I have been telling folks to grab what you can and GO! White folks are going crazy; lynching, looting, shooting... killing." said Mike.

"But why?" asked Jewel.

"I'm not sure, but I heard an incident happened on an elevator with a white woman and a black guy, white folks just got upset and here we are now. Half the town is gone. They're just burning everything." Mike says, while looking down at his battered hands. "Some of us are fighting back, but it's a lot of them. That's why I need ya'll to go."

"What about the restaurant?" asked James Dublin.

Mike looks up at James Dublin, closes his eyes and narrowly shakes his head. He knew how much that restaurant meant to the people in town and more so, how much it meant to the Dublin family.

Maebelle starts to cry hysterically as she says "nooo, no, no, NO!"

"Go, where?" James Dublin asked.

"I've been telling everyone to go about 16 miles up the road, off of highway 18. My great granddad has a house and land out there. We'll take in everyone until we can figure out what to do next," said Mike.

Mike turns to Maddox, he gives Maddox a hug and whispers, "I'll be back to see if you guys are gone. Get your family out... of... here!"

When they released, they stare at each other and exchange head nods. Mike turns to the rest of the Dublin family, smiles and says,

"Everything is gonna be alright. Just... just leave."

Chapter Four

ANOTHER NIGHTMARE

Later that night, James was awakened by voices coming from his father's room. At first, he thought his father was on the telephone. James attempted to ignore the voices. He turned over on his stomach and buried his face into the pillow. However, the sounds continued getting louder and louder. Then he heard his father's voice in a panicked rage. A screaming voice ran through the hallway. James quickly jumped out of the bed, but his left foot was tangled in the sheets. James fell, untangled his foot and sprinted to his father's room, he saw his father sitting on the side of the bed, chuckling and shaking his head. James said, "dad you ok?"

His father out of breath answered, "Yes, I'm okay. Are you okay?"

"Another nightmare?" said James. His father nodded.

"Was it about mom? Asked James.

His father nodded. James walked over to his father and hugged him.

"When will you tell me what happened to mom?" James asked.

"In due time, go back to bed son." said Mr. Dublin.

The next morning, emergency vehicles sped down the street. James woke up from all of the commotion coming from outside. Mr. Dublin had his front door open talking to one of the neighbors. James waited at the top of the stairs, nervous and attentive, listening to his father's conversation. He waited for his father to finish, and then he walked down.

"Dad, what happened?"

"I don't know but if the person is dead, then we'll find out." Mr. Dublin answered

"That's not funny dad," replied James.

They both looked at each other and started laughing.

Later that day while James was at school. Before science class started, all the students gathered in the back of the room discussing what happened to Mr. Darby. Some were laughing and cracking jokes.

"You heard that?"

"Mr. Darby died in a freak accident while in his garage. My father knows the sheriff, he said Darby was on a ladder, fell, and landed on a hammer. Unfortunately, he fell on the pick axe and it went through his temple," one kid said.

"He must have been up pretty high because more than half of the hammer entered his brain," said another kid chiming in.

James stayed quiet and listened. He knew when he would get home that his father would do the honors of preparing his body for the funeral.

"Okay, get to your seats!" shouted Mr. Castle.

While James was in football practice, all he kept thinking about was the discussion in class by the other students. How something was just strange and didn't add up. James was all too familiar with strange things. All the framed pictures of people hung up all around his house. His father says they were good people he knew. Father's nightmares. Sometimes his father would go for a run late in the evening to get his mind off of things.

Chapter Five

WE GO TOGETHER, WE STICK TOGETHER

A thick and heavy cloud of smoke covered the town.

"Jewel, let's go!" shouted Maddox.

"Jewel, you got everything?" asked Maddox. "Yes, hon," she

replies.

"Ma, Dad, let's go!" shouts Maddox.

Suddenly the house is rocked by several explosions.

B-O-O-O-O-M!

B-O-O-O-O-M!

CRASH!

B-O-O-O-O-O-M!

by Henry Charles

Baby James begins to cry hysterically. Screams can be heard from people outside. Vehicles can be heard racing back and forth. The sounds of war: gun shots, explosions, the echoing cries of scared people, pure mayhem! Maddox cracks the front door; opens it wide and walks out onto the front porch. He is amazed in disbelief of what he sees. His town being destroyed, people he knows running with fear in their eyes. The mini skyline which his city formed was now unrecognizable. Buildings, structures, homes, all reduced to rubble.

The height of buildings was replaced by huge tall flames. The night sky engulfed by thick, black smoke, making the moon barely visible. The crisp air consumed by gasoline aroma. Maddox stood motionless, watching as white people looting and destroying his town.

"They killed my baby! They killed my baby!" screamed Mrs. Oliver, as she's being carried away by her sister Ella. Maddox would always sit behind Ella in church, teasing Ella about her various church hats.

One Sunday, Maddox tapped Ella on the shoulder, she leaned back, he whispered,

"Hey, I just prayed to God. I asked him to shrink your hat, so that I can see the whole church service this Sunday. But it didn't work, so can you please take that big ol' fruit basket off yo' head."

Ella whispered back, "boy, hush!" as she giggles.

Another Sunday, Ella reluctantly had her hat off as Maddox sat behind her. Maddox tapped Ella on the shoulder, she leaned back, he whispered, "Hey, can I borrow twenty-two dollars?"

"Why so much?" Ella responded with a grimace.

"Well, two is for the collection plate, twenty is for me," Maddox replied.

Ella turned around, eye-balled Maddox up and down. Turned, sat up in her seat and put on her big church hat.

Maddox whispered, "nooooo, I can't see. I can't see."

Maddox snaps out of it after being violently shaken by the sounds of even louder explosions. This time, it seemed to be coming from the dark skies. Maddox looked up and saw what was a plane. He couldn't believe what he saw next. Descending from the plane were bombs.

"Errrrrrrrrr!" A black pick-up truck comes to a screeching halt in front of the Dublin's house. Maddox takes a cautious step back.

"Aye, ya'll comin'?" shouted the frantic woman driver. "Mike said for us to stop here and get ya'll, ya'll ready?"

Maddox peers into the truck to see who is in it; a bunch of scared black faces. Maddox recognizes the driver. It's Malory Jones, Mike's older cousin. "Yeah, we're coming!" Maddox shouts back at Malory. Maddox shouts at his family, "we got a ride, LETS! GO!" Maebelle is the first to come out of the house. Maddox helps his mother up on the back of the pick-up truck, which also had people hitching a ride. Everyone made room for Mrs. Dublin. They knew the Dublin family and treated them with great respect.

"We can switch places Mrs. Dublin, there's more room over here," one man said as he gave up his comfortable spot on the back of the pick-up. Maddox looked back to the house for his wife and father.

"I ain't got all day Maddie, lets go!" Malory said frantically.

"They're coming. Please! My wife is pregnant."

Malory shakes her head with disgust. "Look, my husband is coming up behind us now. He can take them. He was told by Mike to stop here too before heading to my uncle's manor, just get in," Malory pleads.

"Yeah just get in, son," said James, Sr. as he held baby James.

"Maddox, take your son," he says, as he hands over his grandson, a large satchel and a shotgun.

"Get in the truck!" James, Sr. demanded.

"What? No! We go together, we stick together," suggested Maddox.

"Listen, nothing will happen to your wife, that won't happen to me first," says James, Sr. while loading up his shotgun. "Go with your mother. I heard Malory say there will be another ride coming. Me and Jewel will get on that one!"

"Go on Maddox," says Jewel. "Momma gonna need you."

"Pop! Pop! Pop! Pop! Pop! Pop!"

Everyone on the truck tried to get down as low as they could. Jewel, Maddox and James, Sr. hit the ground hard. Bullets were shot towards the group, hitting the cab of the truck. Malory, looking through the rearview mirror says, "there my baby go! Get in this truck Maddox."

Chapter Six

THE PAIGE ROADSTER

Every Saturday morning, up and down the street. Engine roaring, tires screeching. You knew Todd Macintosh was coming once you heard the engine of his 1919 Paige Roadster roaring. The kids looked up to him a lot. He owned many classic cars from the 1920s. Todd is much older but acted young behind the wheels of his racing cars. All the kids around town felt like he was the coolest adult in town because of his collection of cars. His cars were his prize possession. Everyone knew how much Todd loved his cars.

Mr. Dublin and James were in the front yard doing yard work and could hear the roaring, revving engine of Todd Macintosh racing up the street. Todd zoomed past their house, made a sharp turn right before the light pole and continued to race on down the street. As Todd flew past, James had a grin on his face which quickly disappeared when he saw the look of disgust on his father's face.

"What dad? Why are you looking like that? Don't you like Todd? He's cool!" said James.

"I think he's an idiot," said Mr. Dublin. "Doesn't he know there's kids and elderly people walking around? He's gonna hurt someone driving like that or worse, get himself killed."

"Aww c'mon dad, Todd is cool, you have to admit his car is cool," James replied.

"You kids don't know what cool is," said Mr. Dublin. "What if I started driving the hearse up and down the street, would you think I was cool then?" Mr. Dublin said sarcastically.

Both started laughing hysterically.

by Henry Charles

Chapter Seven

I KNOW WHAT'S IN YOUR HEART

A car can be seen zig-zagging through the street; tires screeching, dodging cars, fire and debris and other projectiles on the road. Maddox got in the back of the truck, deep down he knew he was making a mistake. But he always trusted the words of his father. His father never let him down. Malory pulls off. Maddox looks down at baby James momentarily, then looks up and doesn't take his eyes off of his father and his wife. That was the last time Maddox would see them.

Malory finally reached Jones Manor. She was greeted by relatives, friends and members from town. Not everyone was upbeat. The mood was somber. You could hear the moaning and cries of the women and children.

The men were quiet; mentally and physically fatigued, defeated. The people

lost their loved ones, homes, businesses, valuables, and possessions.

Malory attempts to shift the mood despite knowing the obvious.

"C'mon inside y'all, why is everyone so quiet?" She orders one of

her cousins to help the elderly people off of the back of the truck. "There's

food inside, I know ya'll hungry. I know I am!"

Maddox stood up and carefully jumped off the pickup truck, then

helped his mother down. All while holding his son and gripping the shotgun

his father gave him, with the satchel strapped across his chest. "Mom go

inside," Maddox said.

His mother obliged. "Give me the baby," she replied.

As everyone went inside, Maddox had a terrible feeling in his gut.

He waited and waited and waited. Maddox looked down and realized he

had a leather strap across his chest. He pulled the strap over his head,

kneeled and opened the satchel. It was full of money. Maddox rummaged

through the satchel in disbelief. It was filled with hundred dollar bills and a

few silver and gold coins. Maddox became enraged, he felt guilty for

leaving his wife and father behind.

Malory was in the kitchen holding back tears while she made sure

everyone had a plate of food and was being taken care of. Every now and then she would act as if she was getting things for guests from the basement, but she would go downstairs to cry. She knew something had gone wrong. Her husband Wayne should have been back a long time ago. After all, the joke around town was that Wayne drives like he has cement in his shoes. He can make a one hour drive feel like ten minutes.

Maddox storms into the house and pauses... The mood in the house resembled a funeral repast. Adults crying, talking and whispering. Little kids are not fully understanding the impact of the day; they were playing and running around. Maddox takes a deep breath then shouts, "Malory! Where's Malory!?"

A teenage boy holding a plate of food lifted his hand, barring a fork, hurries and chews his food, swallows, "sh-she's downstairs," he said, then continues to eat. Maddox goes down into the basement. In the corner he sees Malory trying to wipe tears from her face.

"Hey, Maddie," she says.

"I need your keys," Maddox says in a very demanding tone.

"Wait. What?" says Malory.

"I need your keys!" Maddox said even louder.

"I heard what you said, I'm trying to figure out, why you wanna do something so stupid! Don't you see what's going on upstairs?" She says

while gesturing to the ceiling. "My husband is DEAD! You don't have to tell me that."

Maddox looks away as if he wasn't listening. Malory walks over, she reaches up and gently places both of her hands on Maddox's face. In a soft quiet tone she says, "You need to be happy that you still have your mother and your son."

Unfazed Maddox says, "I am. Now, can I have those keys?"

"What are you gonna do?" Marlory shouts while snatching her hands away from Maddox's face. "What are you gonna do? With ONE! GUN!?"

Maddox fires back, "my wife is still out there! My father! Your husband! OUR PEOPLE!"

Maddox startles Malory with his response, She slowly hands Maddox the keys to her pickup truck. As Maddox turns to leave, Malory grabs Maddox's arm. He turns around and she hugs him and begins to cry hysterically. Maddox comforts her, then he makes his way up the stairs. When he opens the door, Maddox is met by all of the men from town. Despite being battered and bruised, they all had stern, angry looks on their faces. Maddox assumed they were going to try to stop him from going back to town. One of the men moved in front of the crowd and said, "We know what you're trying to do."

Maddox shook his head and said, "yall better get outta my way."

Clutching his shoulder, the man said, "Nooo. We want to come with you."

Maddox looks around, he sees the grandmothers, mothers, sisters, wives, aunts and daughters crying. The kids were playing; not caring about what was going on. He smiles and says, "If we all go and don't come back. Who will be here to protect the women and children?"

Without saying any words, the men agreed with Maddox. Maddox went over to his mother. She said, "I know what you are about to do. I know what's in your heart. Just. Come back to me."

He responds, "yes, mom." Maddox hands over the satchel to his mother and kisses his mother and son on the forehead. With the shotgun in tow, Maddox enters the truck and heads full speed towards town. His mind is racing; his thoughts are confused but permeated with pure rage. His heart filled with sorrow, guilt and regret.

As Maddox gets closer to town, he turns the headlights off, pulls the truck over, and parks off the road, out of sight. He begins to run the rest of the quarter-mile into town. He can hear gunshots still going off. Finally, he makes it to his beloved hometown, and it is unrecognizable. Everything seems to be charred. The fires which towered the tall structures earlier that evening had died down. There were dead bodies all over the street. Maddox checked a few of them to see if anyone was alive, but they weren't. The smell of gasoline and smoke suffocated the air. There were groups of white men that congregated around town who seemed to be looking for more black people to harm. Maddox made sure to move as quietly as he could. Maddox finally reached his home. The front door seemed to be knocked off the hinges. The windows throughout the house were smashed and broken. Maddox crouched down and silently moved about, while cautiously calling out to his father and wife. The house had been ransacked and looted; all of the furniture had been turned over and damaged. Everything was on the floor; picture frames, wall units, drapes, paintings, chandeliers, ceiling fans, clocks, mirrors and lamps. Maddox slowly entered the kitchen and it was more of the same. All of the doors on cupboards were open and all of the fine china was all shattered on the floor. The kitchen utensil drawers were open, but no utensils were on the floor. Maddox then realized his mother's favorite china set that was inlaid with solid gold, was not smashed on the floor; they were gone, along with the pure silver utensils.

Chapter Eight

MISSISSIPPI

"Hey brother! I thought you weren't going to make it," said Mike

Jones. Mr. Dublin's long time childhood friend.

"You know I'm always going to be up here, at the same time every month.

But I'm not driving like you, I'm on foot," said Mr. Dublin.

"I see, you still think we're on the football team running laps for

coach Clipp Straughter," jokingly says Mike. "I don't know how you run

10 miles up here every month."

"I'm trying to keep up with my little boy," says Mr. Dublin.

"Little boy? He isn't little anymore. How is he?" asked Mike.

"He's doing real good! Playing ball, he's got the whole town talking about him. He's got a girlfriend too. She's white. Hey, how's Shell and the kids doing?" asked Mr. Dublin.

"They're all doing good." Says Mike, as the smile on his face slowly disappears.

"I'm not gonna be able to make it up here to meet you anymore," said Mike.

"What? Why not?" Mr. Dublin asked.

"You know, we're trying to build our town back to what we had before. I feel like these little rendezvous are pointless. I promised to meet you here in the beginning, every month just to check up on you. But it's almost 20 years! I meet you here so that you can change your mind and move to our new town, but you just don't want to leave that place. I don't know why you're still there. Still living amongst those people; knowing what they did to us! And you sit there and work for them and take care of their dead, like they are sacred people!" shouted Mike.

"You don't understand. M-m-my job isn't done yet," said Mr. Dublin.

"I know, you are too busy mixing with those white folks who destroyed us, who killed us," said Mike.

"Look, I know you're angry, but I can't just up and move because you feel I'm doing something wrong. Remember, I have a son to look after." Mr. Dublin said.

Mike shook his head; turned his back and began walking towards his car. He stops.

"Rochelle and I have a huge barn. If you ever change your mind, you and James are more than welcome," said Mike.

He entered his vehicle and slammed the car door. Mike starts the engine, accelerates; forming a cloud of thick dust that slowly moves towards Mr. Dublin. He just stood there watching as his close friend drove off; unaffected by the dust cloud, Mr. Dublin just stood there.

Mr. Dublin starts to run the ten and a half miles back home. The trail is a grueling path of rough and uneven terrain, steep hills and not to mention the hot Oklahoma morning sun. Mr. Dublin continues to run through his usual path. As Mr. Dublin enters the city limits, he can see his house along with other homes behind it. In the distance he sees his son James talking to two men. But as he gets closer, the more he realizes that the conversation seems more like an altercation. Also, Mr. Dublin notices one of his hogs is down on the ground and not moving; presumably dead and James is furious.

Mr. Dublin recognizes the two men James is arguing with as Matt Parks and his son Matthew. Matt Parks has a reputation for taking things that don't belong to him, or borrowing things and forgetting to return them. Last spring, Mr. Dublin agreed to let Matt borrow a ladder from their shed. Matt used the ladder to patch up the holes on his roof. He did such a good job, people in the town hired Matt to fix their roofs. Matt started his roof fixing business and denied ever borrowing a ladder from the Dublins, even after being asked numerous times to return the ladder. Before that, when Matt Parks and his family were moving into town, he asked Mr. Dublin could he use his nag to haul his carriage to his garage. That would be the last time Mr. Dublin saw his horse alive again. James went to retrieve the horse later that day; Mr. Dublin found the horse dead in the barn the next morning.

The Parks lived a few houses down from the Dublins; James and Mathew attend the same school.

"Here's my dad, we'll see what he has to say 'bout this!" said James.

"What seems to be the problem Matt?" said Mr. Dublin, while slightly panting from his long run.

"No problem here, but your son needs to be taught some manners!" said Matt.

"Dad look at what they did, they killed Mississippi! I was watching them. I watched them go into the barn, shoot her, then carry her out here." James said hysterically.

"That's not true, we were walking and saw Alabama. Oops! I mean Mississippi." Matthew said jokingly. Father and son started laughing at their own joke. Mr. Dublin and James were not amused. Mr. Dublin looked at the trail of blood from Mississippi to the barn.

"Alright, listen. I'm fresh out of hogs and being that we're good neighbors; I thought I'd help myself to your pasture. Especially since you do *such* a great job." said Matt.

Matthew snickered.

James balled up his fists, slightly moves his right foot forward then slides his left foot back, and begins to bite on his bottom lip.

Both men and their sons stood in front of each other as if they were about to brawl. Mr. Dublin and Matt stood equally the same as far as height. Mr. Dublin was much more muscular than Matt.

Matt was similar in size with Mr. Dublin; husky, broad shoulders, like he chopped wood for a living. James and Matthew also were the same height. Matt does odd jobs around the neighborhood and is hardly ever seen without his son Matthew; the two are inseparable. Their hygiene isn't the best; their skin resembles a lightly toasted marshmallow. Matt has a long, thick, dirty, brown beard. Matthew resembles his father but has a head full of hair which he doesn't bother to brush or comb. Matt is married but you wouldn't know he was because he and Matthew are never home. They are usually out on foot excursions. Their expeditions would last for days at a time. Mrs. Parks would often check in with neighbors to see if they had seen or heard from Matt and Matthew, especially when the school called with complaints of Matthew's poor attendance.

It was a battle of opposites; black versus white, smiles versus frowns, good versus bad. Mr. Dublin puts his arm across James' chest and backs his son up.

"Go inside James!" Mr. Dublin orders his son.

"Wh-What-why??"

James sighed with a look of disappointment on his face. Shaking his head, he answers, "Yes dad."

"Goodnight, son!" shouts Matthew.

Mr. Dublin takes two steps towards Matt.

"I suggest you get off of my property now." Mr. Dublin says

sternly.

"Sure, as soon as I get my hog. Uhhhhhhgh!" says Matt as he

bends down and picks up Mississippi's lifeless, bloody carcass.

Mr. Dublin calmly starts walking towards his front door. He could

hear Matthew joking about how they killed Mississippi.

"I told you I could handle a rifle from long range." Matthew says, while

boasting to his father.

Still exhausted from his rendezvous-run, Mr. Dublin slowly walks

up his front steps and before he could fully open the door, he sees James

standing by the doorway. James was upset.

"So we're gonna just let them take from us again, Dad?" James

exclaimed. "They're gonna continue doing this unless we do something!"

Mr. Dublin shook his head.

"Go to your room James." Mr. Dublin said.

"How can we…" Before James could finish his sentence, Mr. Dublin

fiercely cuts him off,

"**NNNOW!**" Mr. Dublin shouted.

The tone of his father's voice frightened James. He never heard his

father speak in such a tone. James' left eye began to water. He didn't want

48

his father to see him cry, so James ran up the stairs as fast as he could. Mr. Dublin closed the front door and walked into the living room. He gazed at all of the faces that were in the picture frames.

James enters his room and slams his bedroom door shut. Tears drop from his eyes, he balls up his right hand into a fist and punches into his left hand twice, the second time, he held his fist in his hand and thinks about what he could have done differently; every time he thought of doing something in retaliation, his father's voice would interrupt his thoughts...

"James, don't do that."

"I taught you better than that, son."

His father's soothing and commanding voice calmed him down. James understood why his father told him to go inside. James got undressed; laid on his bed and went to sleep.

by Henry Charles

Chapter Nine

BLIND TOM

There were no signs of his family, so Maddox made up his mind to

leave; walking through the living room Maddox then realizes his father's

piano was missing. Maddox stopped and stared at the empty space where

his father's Baldwin concert grand piano once stood. The piano was a sight

to be seen; it was the only one of its kind in town, the shiny black painted

wooden panels gleamed when the lights were turned on. James Dublin, Sr.

was a "jack of all trades." He cooked, ran a business, fixed cars, farmed

animals and vegetables and like most of the black residents in town; he

built his house by hand. One thing that made James Dublin, Sr. stick out

was that he knew how to play the piano very well. Maddox remembered how his father would play the piano while he and his mother danced in the middle of the living room. Other times, he would watch his mother dance. The way she moved; so elegantly seemed as if she was floating. Maddox would fall asleep listening to his father play classical music.

Maddox loved hearing his father tell stories of "Blind Tom," whom he learned to play the piano from. Thomas "Blind Tom" Wiggins was an African-American who was born into slavery in the mid-1800s. Tom was born blind and because of this, his slave owner wanted to kill him because he would not be able to perform any slave labor. His life was spared, and as a kid he was allowed to roam the plantation, and that's when he developed the skill of mimicking sound, as well as a passion for music and the piano. At the age of four, Blind Tom had acquired some piano skills by ear, he was then given access to a piano. One year later Tom had composed his first tune. When Tom's slave owner recognized Tom's skills, he allowed Tom to live in a room attached to the house. From there, Tom grew to become one of the best composers of the 19th century.

Maddox's thoughts are rudely interrupted by squeaking brakes and tires dragging on the asphalt. The first thing that popped into Maddox's head was his shotgun, then he realizes he forgot it in the truck. So he inconspicuously runs up the stairs and stops at the top of the staircase listening closely. Maddox makes out about four different voices that are inside of his house. He is convinced that these are the people partly responsible for the chaos and looting.

"Hey! Yo! Chubbs!" One of the men shouts out while entering the Dublin's house.

"We came in here already and y'all took all the silver. Let's go to the Jones' house. That's where everybody went," one man said.

"Let's get Chubbs and go," another man said.

"Hey Todd, can I get one of your cars? You won't be able to drive all of them at once," another voice said jokingly.

"Nope, I Told you guys to follow me. But you wanted to steal little things like watches, spoons and forks," said Todd as he chuckled.

"Are there any more music instruments here? Said another voice.

"Instruments! Are you joining a band or something?" Todd said jokingly and the rest of the guys began to laugh.

"Look, you're gonna have to tell Mrs. Lilly Richardson, we're looting for ourselves. NOT for her!" said another voice.

"Looks like Chubbs had too much to drink," said one of the men.

"I told y'all not to give him that last beer," said Todd.

"I'm having a bad feeling about this. We should go!" said another voice.

"Relax, Bates! We're just looking for things these nice colored folks left behind," said the other voice, while laughing.

"Hey, you think these paintings are worth anything?" said Todd.

Maddox became impatient; he didn't want to stay in the same position listening to the men disrespecting his home any longer; he grew more and more frustrated. Maddox knew he was outnumbered, he was without a weapon not to mention, these people are in his house looting. He knew he had to be careful, the floors upstairs were very creaky and would alert the intruders to his presence.

"You guys didn't have to trash the place," said Bates, as he tried to walk over broken furniture.

"HEY! Isn't this the fried chicken restaurant-family-people's house?" said one of the men.

"Okay, okay, let's go. Let's get Chubbs and get to the Jones house before the others take everything," said Todd.

Maddox was baffled and took a step back. All four men walked over to the staircase and shouted, "CHUBBS! Oh Chuuuubbs! Yo Chubbs! Let's go!"

by Henry Charles

Maddox hears a slow and quiet creak sound behind him. He quickly turned around and it was Chubbs! Six foot four. Heavy-set, brown hair. He was upstairs the whole time drunk and throwing up in the bathroom. He must have passed out. He was standing in the hallway barely able to keep himself up. Maddox quickly thought to himself, this could be his only chance at getting some type up payback without getting caught. Chubbs is drunk and probably won't remember what happened to him. Maddox balled up his right fist and struck Chubbs with a hook. Chubbs didn't know what had hit him, he fell back and made a loud thudding sound. His friends assumed he had too much to drink and took a hard fall in the hallway, they began to laugh shouting, "Ohhh! Chubby-Chubbs!"

Chapter Ten

THE GREATEST HEAVY-WEIGHT CHAMPION

The next morning, James sits up on his bed, checks the time and

realizes he is going to be late for school. James rushes to the bathroom and

takes a quick shower; gets dressed, and starts making his way down the

hallway steps next to his father's room. James peers into his father's room

and notices the bed sheets; crispy clean and untouched. The bed sheets

were pristinely tucked under the mattress still neat from the prior day. He

runs downstairs and heads for the front door when something in his

peripheral vision catches his attention. There's a picture frame missing. All

of the picture frames are lined up neatly, but one is missing. James walks

into the living room and notices his father on the floor, on the other side of the table. His father was asleep; the missing picture frame in his grasp. It was a picture of his mother. James reached down, grabbed the picture and carefully placed it back in its place.

"I'm sorry son..."

James interrupts. "It's okay dad. I know. Plan, plot and strategize. When the time is right, you strike! And you strike hard. They will never know what hit'em."

"Help me up," said Mr. Dublin.

James reaches down for his father's hand and pulls him up.

"Ahh, my leg," said Mr. Dublin.

"what's wrong dad?" James asked

His father's pant leg was torn, with dried blood covering the bottom half.

"Dad are you okay? What happened?" asked James.

"It looks worse than what it is, really. I went for a run last night. I tried to hurdle over a fence, but my back leg didn't clear and my leg scraped the top of the fence. It's really just a long scratch, but my pants just got torn in the process," explained Mr. Dublin.

"Okay, well I'm late for school. I'll see you later Dad." said James. Mr. Dublin yawned, stretched, nodded, waved his hand, laid back down on the floor and went back to sleep.

"Robert Carter?"

"Present!"

"Andre Charles?"

"Present!"

"Timothy Washington?"

"Present!"

"Melanie Dorn?"

"Present!"

"James Dublin?"

"Present!"

"Matthew Parks?

Matthew Parks!" Mr. Smith shouted, looking up to an empty seat.

James turns his head to the right and looks at Matthew's chair. The two often argue in class and sometimes have to be separated to keep from fighting. One day in the cafeteria the boys were debating who was the best boxer. The girls just sat back giggling as the boys were shouting out names of different fighters; Benny Lynch, who was a flyweight, Scottish fighter. Maximillian Adolph Otto Siegfried Schmelling, better known as Max Schmelling, a German heavyweight fighter who reigned in the early 1930s. Barney Ross, an American decorated World War II veteran, who became champion in three different weight classes. William Harrison Dempsey, also known as "The Manassa Mauler," better known as Jack Dempsey. He was an American heavyweight champion who became an icon from the sport of boxing, just to name a few.

James entered the cafeteria, walked over to get his lunch tray and proceeded to the lunch line. He can hear the ruckus from the boys. His intentions were to get his food and sit away from the attention. Because James is the only black student in the school, students always seem to value his input and opinion on everything. James notices that, so he tries to avoid these instances, but it's hard when you tend to stick out like a sore thumb.

"James! James! Get over here!" shouted one of his teammates from the varsity football team. James intentionally sat on the other side of the cafeteria.

"James! C'mon!"

James pretended not to hear his name being shouted across the cafeteria and continued munching on his hamburger. James felt a nudge on his arm.

"I think they're calling you," said Houston Burke.

With a mouth full of food, "nooo, really?" James replied sarcastically, shaking his head.

A few minutes passed when Houston Burke grabbed his milk carton, placed it on his tray, got up and briskly walked away. When he did this, James paused. He knew what was coming. James put his half-eaten hamburger down, took a big deep breath and exhaled. The crowd of boys brought the debate to James. "Jay, I know you heard me maaan," said Josiah Bernard.

"What's up fellas? what is it this time?" asked James as he stood up and faced the crowd of rowdy teens.

"Okay, okay, we're talking about the best boxers!" shouts Josiah. "Who you got James?"

"I bet you he says a colored person," muttered Matthew Parks to Nick Larkins.

James heard Matthew and looked him straight in the eyes and said, "Oh that's easy. The greatest heavyweight champion of all-time. The Brown Bomber." Everyone looked around puzzled.

"Who?"

"Who did he say?"

"What did he say?"

"The brown whuh?"

"Oh excuse me," James said laughing. "Joe Louis!"

The group erupted in a roar. "OHHHHHHHHH!"

"I told you he would pick a colored," Matthew said to Nick.

"Well honestly, I think Joe Louis sucks," shouted Matthew.

"Oooow!" The boys said together.

"Who did you pick?" James replied.

"Max Schmeling! Who put a whoopin' on the Black, oops! I mean your Brown Bomber!" said Matthew while laughing.

"That fight could have gone either way, both fighters went the distance and Joe Louis just ran out of gas," James exclaimed.
"It doesn't matter," said Matthew, "your guy LOST!"

The boys were laughing at James and praising Matthew.
James smiled and sarcastically said, "Wait a minute. I do remember there was a rematch!"

"Did you know about a rematch?" Nick asked Matthew.

"Sh… sure I did," said Matthew. Matthew had no clue of the rematch.

"Joe Louis knocked Schmeling down twice. The second knockdown; Schmeling was out cold. Joe Louis tucked him in like a newborn baby in the first round. The fight was over in juuuuussssst two minutes! After the fight, Schmeling hasn't fought in the United States

since. Joe Louis annihilated him; sent him packing back to Germany!"

James had a big smile on his face. The boys were too ashamed to

laugh at Matthew, they all turned away. But that all changed once Nick

Larkins burst out laughing hysterically. The rest of the boys couldn't hold it

back anymore, there were a few loud snickers until they went into a frenzy.

"Back to Germany!" said Josiah.

"The German Bomber!"

"No! No, no, no…. It's Joe Louis, The German Bomber!"

The boys could not stop heckling. The cafeteria turned into a madhouse of

laughs. Even Houston Burke came back to the table and chimed in, "good

night Maxie!"

"Two minutes! Two minutes!"

Then they started chanting, "Brown-Bom-Mer! Brown-Bom-Mer!

Brown-Bom-Mer!"

Matthew was so mad his cheeks turned bright red. James just

continued to smile showing both rows of his pearly whites at Matthew.

Matthew couldn't take it anymore, he charged at James.

"I'll show you, Aaaaaaarrrgh, I'll get rid of you, just like the

others!" shouted Matthew.

The boys held Matthew back. James didn't understand what Matthew meant by what he said.

"What!? What did you say? What did you say to me?" James charged at Matthew. The cafeteria staff had to hold James back.

PING! PING!

James' thoughts are interrupted by the sound of the bell, alerting the period is over. There was always bad blood between James and Matthew. Just then, James remembered what Matthew said during their altercation. "I'll get rid of you, just like the others." James knew this was something he had to tell his father. It was the final period of the school day. James hurried and packed his things.

"Attention class!" said Mr. Smith, "If any of you see or talk to Mr. Matthew Parks. Tell him he is going to fail my class if he doesn't show up."

James overheard Natalie Oliver say to the group of girls, "I wish I had a father like Matthew, He hasn't been to school all week."

Chapter Eleven

...COLD. LIFELESS. GONE. DEAD.

Maddox takes off. Sneaking into his parent's room, he jumps out of the window and runs off as fast as he could, not looking back. He feels better after unleashing some of his pent up rage on Chubbs. As Maddox gets closer to the truck, he stops dead in his tracks. With his heart beating full of adrenaline, Maddox manages to stand still. He was running so fast he could feel his heart pound through his chest like African drums. He walks backwards and stops. There were tire marks that veered off the road. He follows the tire marks which lead him to a car. The car is riddled with bullet holes. Malory's husband was in the front seat along with two other people, dead. Maddox looks into the back and sees his father cradled over someone; his wife. It seems his father attempted to shield Jewel from the hail of bullets but he was unsuccessful in his attempt. Everyone in the car is cold. Lifeless. Gone. Dead.

Maddox yelled in anguish at the top of his lungs. With both hands he started banging on the roof of the car and continued until he was out of energy. His hands were bloody, numb, bruised and swollen. He only stopped banging because he was exhausted. He was barely able to grip the door handle of the car, which was locked. Maddox painfully made a fist with both hands and began punching the car window until it shattered. He then somberly walked to the truck and drove to the car. Maddox began moving each body onto the back of the bed of the pick-up truck. With each body he moved, Maddox cried uncontrollably, whimpering in excruciating pain from using his badly battered hands. When all of the bodies were loaded into the truck bed, Maddox drove off.

Maddox finally reaches Jones Manor. The windows throughout the home were dark. Mentally and physically exhausted, Maddox shifts the gears into park and just sits in the pick-up with the engine running. His head begins to nod behind the wheel. As Maddox falls asleep, he is awakened by the heavy front door slamming shut and the hysterical screams of Malory as she is rummaging through the bodies on the truck bed, only to find her husband lying there motionless. The lights begin to turn on in each window of the house. People are coming outside to see what's causing all the commotion. Other women begin to scream and holler, some holding their hands up to their mouths; crying in disbelief as they see the bodies. More people start to come outside to console a shaken Malory, they bring her inside. Three men approached Maddox to help him out of the vehicle, one man reached into the truck and turned the ignition off. They notice he is in a state of shock and exhaustion, the men carry Maddox inside. Everyone enters the home, and just like that... it is quiet again.

Chapter Twelve

NATIVE SON

The next morning, James hit the door running with his routine jog to school. James noticed sirens coming from the school's direction. The sirens are getting louder and louder and he gets close to school. As James sprints, a sheriff's vehicle speeds right past him. James finally arrives at school and notices something strange. Students were huddled up in hallways, whimpering. He didn't bother to stop and asked anyone what was wrong. James speed walked through the vacant hallways, which were always crowded with students and teachers. James made it to class but the classroom was empty. He didn't care; he knew he was late and since no one was in class he figured he was on time. James sat down panting The whimpering in the hallway turned into a loud ruckus. Suddenly students started running down the hall in packs. James just ignored it. Still panting, James held his breath to listen to the numerous odd sounds that were coming from the hallway. Finally, it hit James: something was wrong. James stood up and walked to the doorway. He looked to the left, then to the right. James heard running footsteps coming from around the corner. It sounded like a stampede, but it was only Michael Williams and a few players from the junior varsity football team. "Mike, what's going on? Where's everybody?" asked James.

"Whussup Jay? School is cancelled. You didn't hear!?" Michael burst out, as James exchanged their special hand-shake, which only players on the football team knew. Two high fives and a fist bump.

Michael Williams is a 6'3" 254lb senior; starting right guard. He is the reason why James is able to scamper for so many yards during their games. Michael and James are very good friends on and off the field. "Hear what?" asked James.

"The Smith Brothers. Alexander and Malachi Smith; they got attacked by a pack of wolves!" exclaimed Michael.

"So why is school cancelled?" asked James.

"Apparently they must have been trying to escape the attack and ran through the football field, but they got mauled. I hear body parts are scattered on the fifty-yard line! Why do you think classes are empty? Everyone is outside!" said Michael.

Their conversation is interrupted, "YOO! Mike! You coming?!" shouted Alfred Snell.

Michael turned towards Alfred and took two lunging steps, then remembered he was talking to James. Michael turns to James with his arms out to by his side, "C'mon Jay, you can look from the window and see everything!"

The two took off like they were competing in the forty-yard dash. They reached the huge window at the end of the hallway but had to get past the crowd of sobbing girls, along with amazed and shocked boys.

"Too many people here," Said James.

"I got you Jay. Okay people, MOVE!" shouted Michael, the crowd parted.

"That's Malachi at the goal post," said Michael, as he points out the window. "He got chewed up pretty bad. Aaaaand that right there and right there and right there and right and right there and riiiiiiiiiiiight over there is Alexander." Michael said jokingly.

James wasn't laughing. He knew of Alexander and Malachi. They were much older than he was; the two brothers owned a mechanic shop in town. He always remembered the first time he met Alexander and Malachi Smith; it wasn't a pleasant encounter. He remembers vividly walking to school one morning passing the mechanic shop. Alexander and Malachi Smith were out front drinking beers and working on Mrs. Poole's pick-up truck. Their conversation came to an abrupt end as James walked by. He could feel the cold stares coming from both men as he looked back. James wasn't sure what was being said, but he could hear them whispering, then bursting out in laughter as he walked past. This became a constant thing every morning, but it just got worse as time went on. It went from whispers to laughing out loud, to throwing empty beer bottles at James and calling him, "boy," "coon" and other racial slurs. James never thought anything about it. He felt Alexander and Malachi were just miserable old drunks who would never amount to nothing outside of being mechanics.

Since school was canceled, James decided to go home. He began walking down the hall. "Hey James! Hold up!" James turns around. It was Heather. She was sprinting down the hallway.

"Can you believe what happened to the Smith brothers?" Asked Heather as she kissed James on the right cheek.

"Yeah. It's crazy," James replied.

"Sooo..." Heather said with a big smile on her face. "There's no school today, what are you going to do?"

"I'm just gonna head home," James said uninterestedly, "come by tomorrow." James was really bothered by what he had just witnessed. "Okay, I will," Heather replied.

Later that night, James was in the living room reading his book in the den when his father came home.

"James?" Mr. Dublin shouted.

"Yes, dad!" James shouted back.

"Just checking to see if you're home," said Mr. Dublin.

Mr. Dublin goes upstairs into the bedroom. Changes his clothes then makes his way downstairs into the kitchen. He makes a sandwich and sits down at the kitchen table. James enters the kitchen, kisses his father on the forehead, and leans back on the kitchen counter.

"What are you reading?"

"The book you gave me. *Native Son*," James says.

"Ahh, how do you like it so far?" asked Mr. Dublin.

"I like it a lot. I can't seem to put the book down. I felt bad for Bigger and his family."

"What about Bigger and his family?" asked Mr. Dublin.

"Why does a family have to live in poverty? Why does Bigger have to go work for a white man? Why couldn't they build a business like you did? I look at it like this, Bigger is doing and thinking these bad things because he is being brought up in a bad environment. So, he's being forced to do wrong, because he wants a good life, but ends up making bad decisions. Who wants to live among rats?" James explains while shaking his head. "I'm at the part where Mrs. Daulton enters the room and Biggers is trying to keep Mary quiet with the pillow."

"As human beings, we cannot help the environment in which we are brought up in. Bigger made his choices. They weren't wise choices, but he made his choices and mistakes along the way. Sometimes people are pushed to do bad things, but that does not make them *bad people*."

"Dad, Bigger killed Mary!" James said laughing.

"Yes, but he was just trying to keep her quiet, it *was* an accident," explained Mr. Dublin. "Do you know what they would have done to a black man caught in a white girl's room?"

"He's still a killer!" James says while giggling.

The two continue to go back and forth debating on Bigger's intent and his actions, when suddenly a snapped branch right outside the kitchen window brings father and son to an immediate halt. No words had to be spoken. An intruder was on their property, moreso, right outside the kitchen window. Mr. Dublin stood up almost simultaneously with the sound of the branch. He and James made eye contact. Mr. Dublin nodded slightly giving James a signal. James displayed his athletic ability, bolting through the kitchen and up the stairs. He dashed into his father's bedroom and shut the door. Behind the door, James began to push against the wall with both hands as hard as he could. After three hard thrusts, the wall unlatched. James opened the secret compartment; inside was a cache of weapons and ammunition. James grabbed the Browning Superposed shotgun.

With no street lights, evenings were pitch black, and the moon provided the only source of light. Despite this, Mr. Dublin clearly saw the silhouette of a man, outlined by the moonlight standing outside of his kitchen window. The man took off running to the left, toward the back of the house. Mr. Dublin dashed through the back door of the house to cut the intruder off. The intruder was very fast, but Mr. Dublin was gaining right behind him. Both men were running full speed, until Mr. Dublin leaped forward and tackled the intruder. Both fell onto the soft grass. Mr. Dublin quickly mounted the intruder and began striking him with hard fists and elbows. With every hit Mr. Dublin can be heard, "Umpf! Umpf! Umpf!"

The intruder managed to block most of Mr. Dublin's attacks. While on his back, the intruder planted both feet and thrusted his hips upward, shoving Mr.Dublin off.

"You're weak but you still have that speed I see," the intruder said while laughing and trying to catch his breath.

"Mike? Is that you?" asked Mr. Dublin.

"Yeah it's me." said Mike.

Mr. Dublin became enraged. "What are you doing outside of my kitchen window!?" shouted Mr. Dublin.

"I *always* come by to check on you two," Mike says. "Calm down. I heard people in the town were getting killed…"

Mr. Dublin interrupts Mike, "Yeah, so!"

"SO! The last time people in this town were being killed, it didn't pan out for *our* people!" said Mike. "I've been here a few nights checking up on you and James. Making sure you two are alright."

"As you can see, we are fine. Now get out of here before James sees you."

"Huh? I can't see my nephew?" asked Mike.

"No! Not like this. I don't want him thinking his uncle Mike is sneaking around peepin' through people's windows at night," said Mr. Dublin.

"DAAAAD!" James can be heard from the other side of the house.

"I'm back by the pasture!" Mr. Dublin shouts back. "Alright, that's him, get outta here." said Mr. Dublin.

"We'll catch up," said Mike. "You know, your son was right."

"About what?" asked Mr.Dublin.

"About Bigger. No matter why he did it. He's still a killer," said Mike.

Mr. Dublin giggled, shaking his head as he watched his old friend run backwards disappearing into the night. James can be heard running towards his father.

"Who was it?? James asked, with his arms out wide, with a shotgun in one hand trying to catch his breath.

"It was a stupid deer. I ran after it just for the fun of it and it took off. I'm getting old."

"A deer?" James said inquisitively.

Attempting to change the subject. Mr. Dublin said, "I knew you were gonna come out here with *that* shotgun. Of all the guns, you always grab this one."

"What can I say, I have good taste," says James.

Mr. Dublin put his arm around James' shoulder and the two walked back to the house.

Chapter Thirteen

FOOD FOR THE SOUL
II

As Maddox slept, he felt something crawling up his upper lip and near his nostrils. In an attempt to swat it, he unsuccessfully slaps himself on the nose, then quickly sits up.

"I told you he's not dead!" says a little girl, holding a twig.

"C'mon, momma said to tell her when he wakes up," said a little boy.

As they raced out of the room, they waved at Maddox and said, "byyyye!"

"MOMMMA! HE'S UP!" HE'S UP!" they both shouted as they raced down the hall, then stomped down the stairs.

Maddox laughed. Then he got quiet, thinking of his family, he began to cry thinking about his father and his beloved wife Jewel; and his unborn child. He wipes his tears with his carefully bandaged hands. Moments later, Malory walks in with a serving tray. "Hey Maddox! I hope you're hungry. I KNOW you're hungry," she said, as she placed the tray on the foot of the bed.

She walked over to the closet and pulled out a small folding table and placed it in front of Maddox. Then placed the tray on the table. Maddox looks down at the tray; two generous portions of country fried steak, a mound of garlic mashed potatoes with bits of red potato skins, bright, sweet green peas, and a lightly toasted, golden yellow, corn on the cob with a glass of milk. Utensils; heavy-silver, pristine and shiny, neatly wrapped in a silk cloth.

"I didn't think you were gonna get up today," said Malory. Maddox smirked.

"That's why I had the kids checking on you, I was just gonna let you sleep. I have something to tell you, buuuuut I'll wait until you are done eating."

"Tell me now," says Maddox.

"No!" She said with conviction. "You need to eat. You've been through a lot. Eat!" says Malory.

Maddox lifted his bandaged hands. "You did this?" he asked.

"Yes, it's the least I could do, y'know," she says. "When you're done, I'll be down stairs."

Maddox looks down at his plate of food which was very tempting, but he couldn't eat. He was still in pain from seeing his family dead. He had no appetite, but knew he had to eat something. He lowered his head into the plate of food, closed his eyes and inhaled deep. Maddox thought of how his parents prepared their dishes. Maddox enjoyed the food prep. Cutting and slicing fresh vegetables, mincing the garlic, masterfully trimming the fat from the meat. He inhaled deeper a second time; he could smell the aroma from the country fried steak, it quickly reminded him of his mother and father's cooking. He snatched up a steak with his bare hands and began eating like he had never seen food before. He took a sip of milk then continued devouring the steak, then moved on to the vegetables until the food was gone.

Chapter Fourteen

A GOLD RING

Mr. Dublin was in the kitchen when James came home from school. "Dad you home?" shouted James.

"Yes son, in the kitchen." replied Mr. Dublin.

"How was school?" his father asked.

James opened the refrigerator door and replied "Eh, it was okay." He grabbed the bottle of milk and began drinking from the bottle. Mr. Dublin plucked James behind his ear and said, "get a glass."

James laughed.

"Dad, I wanted to ask you something,"

"Okay," Mr. Dublin replied.

"I got into it with Matthew…"

Mr. Dublin interrupted, "you mean Parks!?"

"Yes, but let me finish," said James. "We got into an argument and in the midst of other things being said, Matthew said to me, *I'll get rid of you, just like the others*. I thought it was a strange comment to say. Who are the *others*?"

Mr. Dublin paused, before he could say anything, there was a loud bang and then a soft knock at the door.

"I'll get it," said James, as he exits the kitchen, heading to the front door. "Dad it's for you!" James shouted.

Mr. Dublin heads to the front door. It's Mrs. Parks, the wife of Matt Parks. The two exchange greetings at the door.

"Hi Helen."

"Hello Maddox."

"Please, come inside," said Mr. Dublin.

"No, I'm not going to be long. I believe this is yours." said Helen, as she gestures to the ladder.

"Yes, but did you carry this here all by yourself?" Mr. Dublin said in disbelief. Helen nodded. "There is a lot I do by myself. Which is also why I am here. Have you seen my two knuckleheads, Matt and Matthew?

They're gone again and I have been going door-to-door asking if anyone has seen them. This is probably the longest they have been missing without checking in..."

Helen is interrupted by James as he sprints down the stairs and shoots out the front door.

"Hi Mrs. Parks! bye Mrs. Parks! Dad, I'm going to the pasture," says James.

"Wait, I thought you wanted to talk?" said Mr. Dublin.

"We'll talk later!" shouts James.

Helen giggles and shakes her head. "Boys will be boys," she says tearfully as she begins to cry. "The schools been calling, I don't know what to do. I feel it in my gut, something is wrong. I am also here because I want to apologize for what my husband has done to you; this ladder, the horse, the window, your hog, the burning cross. I'm truly sorry."
"The burning cross was Matt?" asked Mr. Dublin. Helen nods.

"It's okay," Mr. Dublin says while smiling. "I accept your apology and if I see your boys I'll tell them you're looking for them." Mr. Dublin gives Helen a hug.

"Thank you," says Helen as she walks away still shaken.

Mr. Dublin puts the ladder into the foyer, shuts the front door and walks into the kitchen when he hears another knock at the door. Immediately he thinks of Helen and what she is going through and hurries to the door.

"Coming Helen," Mr. Dublin says as he opens the door.

"Mr. Dublin! How are you?" asked sheriff Bates.

With a straight face Mr. Dublin replies, "I'm well, everything is good. No complaints."

Sheriff Bates forcefully walks in and passes Mr. Dublin, goes through the foyer looking up at the tall ceilings and enters the living room. He stands in an amazement similar to his daughter gazing at the photos on the wall.

"I came by because of all the deaths going on in town. Just checking on you and everyone else in town. People are afraid. They believe these deaths are not accidents but murders," said sheriff Bates as he bends over to look at a picture.

"Murders?" asked Mr. Dublin.

"The world famous Cotton Club," said sheriff Bates. "Uh, yeah. Remember Todd Macintosh? That fool. Lord knows I told him to slow down. His car wreck wasn't caused by his senseless driving as most people thought. Someone tampered with his break line. The Smith brothers; they were not mauled by wolves like the school kids are saying. Someone hacked them up pretty good. Mrs. Richardson, she was laying at the bottom of her staircase. At her age, any fall from those stairs would kill her," he said laughing.

"But after her son Peter died in the war, she told me she never went upstairs. She just lived downstairs. Then she dies from falling down the stairs. She said she would never go up those stairs, *ever.* I guess it's true what they say about old people. They are stubborn," Sheriff Bates says while he continues to laugh.

"Yes, her bruises and broken bones were consistent with a fall. Why are you telling me this, Sheriff?" asked Mr. Dublin.

"Well, I grew up with these people and I thought you could give me some advice on how you cope, being that you went through something similar," said Sheriff Bates.

"I can't tell you what to do, sheriff, but I pray," says Mr. Dublin.

"You pray? What do you pray for?" asked Sheriff Bates.

"I pray for forgiveness," replied Mr. Dublin. "Sadly. Life goes on."

"Sadly it does," says Sheriff Bates. "I also came by to see how you're doing, being that it's almost the... y'know, anniversary."

"Anniversary? Is that what you call it? Asked Mr. Dublin?

"Well yeah what would you call it? ask Sheriff Bates.

"Nothing. Just another day," said Mr. Dublin. "Are we done here?" he asked sternly.

Sheriff Bates looks down at Mr. Dublin's left hand and notices a shiny, wide, gold ring. He turns around and heads for the front door. "I see you still wear your ring," said Sheriff Bates.

"Yeeeah. I continue to wear the ring because of the anniversary," Mr. Dublin said sarcastically.

Sheriff Bates sensed tension. "Look, I just came by to see if everything is okay.

"If that's all, you will have to excuse me, I have a lot of work to finish," said Mr. Dublin.

Chapter Fifteen

MAN'S PEAK

Maddox feels much better, stands up, stretches, and makes his way

downstairs. He takes his time walking through Jones Manor. It was

beautiful. All the doorknobs are made of solid gold, the wooden floors are

so shiny they look wet, it seems as if they were just waxed. The ceilings are

very high and have fancy ceiling fans. There are pictures hung all through

the hallway in picture frames. The pictures were of black people in the field

smiling, picking cotton, reading books, babies, children, men and women;

there was a picture of a white man in the middle of a crowd of black

people. As Maddox reaches the end of the hallway, he sees a huge, thick

picture frame, with a picture of a white man. Centered at the bottom of the

picture frame was a rectangular gold plated. Engraved it said, "Jiminy

Jones," in big letters. Centered under it, "A good man, with a good heart. God has an angle."

The property originally belonged to Jiminy Jones; a wealthy, white slave owner who would buy as many slaves as he could and allowed them to live free in his house. He would try to buy and keep enslaved families together, rather than buy one and let others split the families apart. If this happened, he would later track the buyer of the slave and make them a counteroffer. Later, people at the auction found out what Jiminy Jones was up to and banned him from the auctions. However, he was very wealthy, he would knowingly pay two or three times over the going rate for a slave. He knew they were trying to deter him from bidding, but that didn't stop him. He believed slavery was wrong and that Jesus would return to punish all those who had taken part in such a cruel and heinous act. In those days, slaves took on the last names of their slave owners. When Jiminy Jones died in the late 1890s, he left all of his property and possessions to his good friend, whom he bought at a slave auction; Gray Jones. The grandfather of Mike Jones. The two became best friends over the years. The property has been passed down from generation to generation in the Jones family.

Maddox notices it is very quiet. No is in the house. He hears voices coming from outside the house. The voices get a little louder as he reaches the bottom of the staircase. Maddox sees more pictures throughout the house. Maddox looks out the window and sees everyone outside with their heads down. He assumes they are holding a vigil for those who lost their lives. He sees his best friend Mike; Malory sees Maddox and acknowledges him with a wink. But he stays inside, he doesn't want to interrupt the procession. Maddox is admiring the home. There are pictures everywhere. It brings a smile to his face.

Finally, it is over. The group starts to enter the house. People coming in see Maddox, they are smiling and nodding to him.

One lady walks over to him with tears in her eyes, "They killed my son, but you brought him back to me, we had a good service for him. Thank you."

She gave Maddox a big hug. Others walked pass padding him on the shoulder as they walked past. Maddox was confused, he felt as though he failed. Mike rushes up to Maddox and playfully punches him in the stomach several times, Maddox clenches his abdomen as the two exchange laughs and hugs. Malory stands off to the side with her arms crossed shaking her head.

"Maaan take those bandages off!" says Mike. "What were you punching, the pillow?"

Maddox shoots back. "No, I was punching your rock shaped head!"

"They were right!" Malory interjects. "You two can't seem to be serious about anything, I swear!"

"Okay, okay," says Mike.

"Maddox, we need to hurry and bury your folks. They're turning blue," Malory says quietly.

Maddox nods.

"A-a-a-and, I am sorry," a broken Malory says as she begins to cry.

"What? Mike, what is she crying about?" asked Maddox.

"Your mother. Maebelle passed away shortly after you left," said Mike.

"Where's James!?" Maddox says quickly.

"Don't worry," Mike says, as he puts his hand on Maddox's shoulder. "We're taking good care of him, and that satchel that your mother had. We have it. No one touched a DIME!"

"We dug up three holes for you out back. When you're ready, we can have a service for them too," Malory said.

"Out back?" Maddox said, puzzled. "For what?"

"So you can bury your family," said Mike.

"No offense. But I'm not burying my family here," Maddox says angrily. "My family and I didn't live here. I'm burying my family at our home."

"You got away last night, but those people will kill you if you go back." Mike says pleading with his best friend. "Don't be foolish, we can start over again and..."

"And WHAT!?" Maddox shouts as he gets in Mike's face. "What if they do the same thing again, HUH!? We're supposed to run and keep running?"

Mike steps a little closer to Maddox with their nose touching and says, "you better get outta my face."

Everyone stopped their chattering. Even the kids halted their horsing around. The mood in the living room was tense. Attempting to hold back tears, Malory comes in between them.

"We're not supposed to be fighting each other," she says. "We're family and you two are like brothers."

As she separates them. They realized how silly they were acting and began looking away from each other and started laughing. The kids start playing again and the adults carry on with their discussions. Mike

quietly walks away.

"Do you have a shovel?" Maddox asked Malory.

"They're all outside, you can't miss 'em."

"Okay," says Maddox. "Oh, one more thing. Can you please look

after James? I'll come for him in a few days."

"Sure," replied Malory.

Assured that his son would be safe. Maddox quickly headed

towards the front door when his right arm is yanked back. It was Mike.

"Give me your word," said Mike. "Every first of the month, we

meet at Old Man's Peak starting next month.

"Why?" asked Maddox.

"To keep me from going back there and looking for you," said

Mike.

Maddox bit his lower lip and nodded. The two shook hands and

hugged. "Man's Peak!" Maddox replied as he walked out of the front

door.

Chapter Sixteen

FOOD FOR THE SOUL
III

James is awoken by the sweet aroma of sizzling bacon and cheese grits, which puts a smile on his face. Mr. Dublin's cooking skills were passed down from generation to generation. You name it, his father can make it. The smile on James' face slowly goes away. James is content. Today will be the day he will demand his father to tell him what happened to his mother. James walks to the bathroom, starts brushing his teeth and begins pondering. In his head, James begins to play out different scenarios of how the conversation would go. Each and every situation he thought of he could only laugh and shake his head. Hungry and anxious, James hurries downstairs.

"Hey dad, good morning," says James as he sits at the kitchen table.

"Mornin', son," said Mr. Dublin. "Do you want a lot?"

"Of course," says James. "I smelled that bacon in my sleep!"

Mr. Dublin laughs. "Here you go," Mr. Dublin said while he ruffled the crown of James' hair. Kissed him on the forehead and placed a big plate of cheese-grits, fluffy scrambled eggs with chopped onions, green and red peppers and spinach, four thick strips of smoked honey-bacon, two moist buttermilk biscuits in front of James.

James thought to himself this is the perfect time to ask about his mother. But he didn't want to be turned down by his father for the hundredth time, so he decided to leave it alone. He picked up a strip of bacon and began to eat. Mr. Dublin walked over to the refrigerator, grabbed a pitcher and poured fresh squeezed lemonade into James' favorite mug and placed it on the table.

"Are you doing anything today?" his father asked.

James had a mouth full of eggs and biscuits. Without being disrespectful and talking with his mouth full, James just shook his head.

"Great. When you're done eating, come downstairs. I need to talk to you," his father said.

After James got done eating, he washed the plate and utensils and put the leftover breakfast away. He made his way downstairs to the basement. Mr. Dublin was putting together another picture frame. He carefully hammered a nail into a narrow piece of wooden frame. He heard James walking behind him.

"Hey dad. What's up?" asked James.

"Have a seat son."

James sat on a stool his father made. Mr. Dublin stopped hammering, still holding the hammer, he put both hands down by his side. James waited for his father to initiate the conversation. It is silent.

"At night I can't sleep. I toss and turn. Inflamed crosses in the dark, nightmares of bodies being burned," Mr. Dublin says while shaking his head.

"Um, I don't get it Dad," said James.

Chapter Seventeen

SMELLS LIKE SMOKE

Heather makes it to the Dublin's house. She reaches for the doorknob and enters the home through the huge, black, unlocked front door.

"James... Mr. Dublin?" she calls out calmly, as she walks into the dining room area where she again begins to gaze at the pictures on the wall. Her eyes begin to wander from picture frame to picture frame. Imagining she was in each photo; mimicking poses and facial expressions. She was having fun, laughing at herself being silly. Suddenly, Heather began to hear voices. She paid them no mind. She knew it had to be James talking to his father; Mr. Dublin. As she continued to prance in front of the photos however, Heather couldn't help but notice a voice getting louder and louder. It was the shouting of Mr. Dublin, a tone of his she had never heard before. Heather started to make her way over to the basement door to eavesdrops on the conversation.

"But why, dad? I just don't understand, w-w-what did they do to you?" cries James.

"What did they do to ME?!" Mr. Dublin shouted. "What did they do to us? They killed US! They destroyed our city! Then they took it over like it was nothing. This was OUR city! We built it! We built this place together, with blood, sweat and years. In just a few days they took it over by starting a riot that killed many of our people. The ones who managed to survive left everything behind; their homes, their possessions, their businesses, EVERYTHING!"

Mr. Dublin paused to collect himself and laughed. "Why do you think I run a funeral home son? I stayed behind to bury the dead. Our family; grandpa, grandma, your mother. She was pregnant," Mr. Dublin says while wiping his tears. "Our friends. OUR PEOPLE! I buried them all."

"Those are the people in the picture frames," said James after making the connection. Mr. Dublin nodded.

"After the riots, those white people saw I was the only negro left. They figured I wasn't a threat. So, they let me be. Some thought I was crazy. I went from home to home collecting bodies. I cleaned them up well to give them a proper burial. After that, I began to collect all the pictures I could gather. I made the frames by hand.

James walked over to his father and hugged him.

"People are pushed to do bad things, but that does not make them bad people."

"What did you say, son?" asked Mr. Dublin.

"That's what you said. When we were talking about Bigger," James said. "You killed them. You killed those people dad!"

"Yes. I did." said Mr. Dublin. "Every time I went out for a jog."

James was shocked. "The Smith brothers?"

Mr. Dublin nodded.

"I knew what those two were doing to you. They did the same to me. The harassment and the stares," Mr. Dublin said with a grimace on his face.

"They're always intoxicated, they like to cut through the football field. I ambushed them. They tried to fight back. I was toying around with

Alexander and he managed to cut my leg," Mr. Dublin snickered. "Then, I

cut them into pieces!"

A teary-eyed Heather heard enough, and she ran home as fast as

she could.

"Todd Macintosh?"

Mr. Dublin nodded.

"You know those fancy fast-cars he was driving? All stolen. The

cars belonged to Chavis Dogger. He loved cars. Mr. Chavis owned the only

car dealership in town. Everyone bought their cars from 'Dog.'" Mr.

Dublin said, shaking his head. "Tampering with his brakes was easy. I

knew with the way he drives, it was going to be simple."

"Ol' Mrs. Richardson?"

Mr. Dublin nodded.

"She's the cause of all this!" Mr. Dublin sounded enraged. "She

lied and said a black man tried to rape her... on an elevator! When a young

black man just tripped into the elevator, bumping into her. But those white

people were always looking for something to use against us as an excuse, to

do us blacks harm. They formed a mob and that was it. That was it! She

had people doing her bidding for her. She paid people to loot for her during

the riot," Mr. Dublin said with disgust.

"It took her long enough to come up those stairs. When she finally did come up, she knew why I was there. I guess I startled her. She fell down those stairs on her own," Mr. Dublin said laughing, which he quickly stopped once he saw James wasn't.

"Mr. Darby? The Parks?"

Sniff, sniff.

"Do you smell that?" asked Mr. Dublin. "Smells like smoke. Do you have anything on the stove?"

"No. I put all the food away," said James.

Smoke began to travel down into the basement. Mr. Dublin and James quickly ran upstairs. When they opened the door, smoke was everywhere, but there was no fire in sight. The two began to cough. Mr. Dublin went for the front door. To his surprise, their house was totally surrounded by an all white mob spearheaded by Sheriff Bates along with a crying Heather by his side. All the members of the mob were armed with either a pistol, shotgun, rifle or a rope. They were ready for a public lynching. Molotov cocktails were being hurled at the roof of the Dublin's home.

"Mr. Dublin!" Shouted sheriff Bates into the megaphone. "We got you surrounded. Come on out and meet your fate. We know what you've done."

"Ehhh, enough with all this talking," said Lang Curry as he fired his rifle, nearly striking James. Mr. Dublin and James ducked back into the house and shut the door. That one shot triggered the mob to riddle the house with bullets. Mr. Dublin and James layed down.

Mr. Dublin shouted, "Stay down! Stay down!"

"What are we gonna do Dad?" cried James as he continued to cough. "Dad I don't wanna die! I don't wanna die!"

"Stay down, crawl into the basement," said Mr. Dublin.

"Why are we throwing cocktails at the roof, instead of just burning the whole house down, sheriff?" Asked Lang Curry, as he reloaded his rifle.

"We want them alive. But that might not happen because of you!" Sheriff Bates shouted.

Lang replied, "They'll come out, no one can breathe in all that smoke."

"They'll come out," said sheriff Bates as he nods. "If they don't, then they are sure to burn in the fire."

Bullets continue to rip apart the already burning home. The roof caves in and the mob began to cheer. More cocktails were thrown, and the mob moved in closer and closer. Everyone was watching the perimeter of the house to make sure no one escaped. Fire trucks arrived, but Sheriff Bates commanded them to stand down. He and the mob wanted the house to burn completely. The second level of the Dublin home caved in and collapsed into the first level. Finally, the rest of the home crumbled into the basement level. A few small explosions went off in the home. This drove the mob crazy as they cheered.

The huge Dublin house which once stood as a cornerstone in the early 1920s is now reduced to rubble. A few hours passed, and the mob continued to celebrate, as they fired shots in the air and danced around the house like a bonfire. Sheriff Bates signaled to the firefighters to put out the rest of the fire. He also ordered the mod to keep a look out for what may look like a body.

"Hey Sheriff!" shouted one of the deputies. "I think you need to come see this." The mob rushed over to the deputy. Sheriff Bates carefully walked over and to his surprise, there were two unrecognizable, charred, swollen bodies stuck together. The mob began kicking and spitting on the corpses. One body appeared to be Mr. Dublin, bigger and wider than the other body. The slender, shorter body seemed to be James.

"I know they were in the house, but how do we know it's them, sheriff? Says Carson Waite.

Sheriff Bates kneeled down and ripped the two bodies apart. He then turned over the bigger body which had been laying its side. He forcefully pulled the left arm up; tearing flesh, which was burnt-stuck to its torso. Most of the mob onlookers looked away, but most of them were amused at such a gruesome scene as if they had done this before.

"What is he doing?" one person whispered.

After a few more tugs, Sheriff Bates bent the arm back in an awkward position.

"CRACK-CRACK!"

Sheriff Bates was able to look at the left hand of Mr. Dublin; where he saw the wide gold wedding band he had seen days before. He smirked and whispered. "I've got you!"

He stood up and faced the mob, "here lies the murderer! And his son!" Sheriff Bates declared. "We no longer have to live in fear!"

The crowd erupted in a loud roaring cheer as they continued to beat the corpses and continued shooting their guns through the night.

Chapter Eighteen

A NEW BEGINNING

"Rochelle, can you pour two glasses of orange juice for me sweetie? Thank you," Mike says to his wife.

She pours orange juice into two tall glasses and places them on a serving tray.

"Here you go Honey," said Rochelle.

"Did Robert get back from the barn yet?" asked Mike.

"No," replied Rochelle.

The back kitchen door squeaks open and slams shut, it's Robert.

"You brought the food into the barn, son?" asked Mike.

"Yes dad," replied Robert.

"I forget to give you the drinks," said Mike. "Can you bring the tray with the orange juice too, please."

"No problem, Dad," says Robert.

Robert grabs the tray and heads for the door, stops and turns to his father.

"Hey Dad, who are those two guys in the barn anyway?" asked Robert.

Rochelle walks over to Mike and puts her arm around him and says,

"they're family."

THE END

ABOUT THE AUTHOR

Henry Charles was born in Manhattan, New York in 1978. Later Henry and his family moved to Far Rockaway, Queens, in 1982. As a kid, Henry collected sports cards, comic books, newspapers and the 'Sports Illustrated' magazines.

Living in Far Rockaway meant living near the Rockaway beaches. When Henry was eleven years old, he had a near death experience. While at the beach with friends, he went into the ocean water alone. Henry nearly drowned. Henry was pulled underwater by a rough undercurrent. Henry was scared, when asked how did you survive? Henry responded, "I couldn't swim, I gave up. I knew for sure I was going to die. I went under water three times, each time I came up, I was screaming for help. But my friends were too far to hear or see me. So, I stopped trying to fight. I came up one last time and took a deep breath and let myself go. I didn't move, I was waiting for the inevitable. Then I felt a wave push me forward, towards shore. I held my breath, stayed still and let the waves push me until I felt the sand under my feet. God was on my side."

Growing up in New York City in the 1980s many considered graffiti as littering or defacing property. However, Henry considered it to be art and fell in love with art. That's when Henry developed a passion for drawing. Henry didn't have a drawing pad, so he would take printing paper from school to draw his pictures.

After graduating from high school in 1996, Henry attended Jackson State University in Jackson, Mississippi, where he pursued his passion for art; majoring in art/graphic design. Henry graduated from Jackson State University with a B.A. in 2002 and made the Dean's List. Shortly thereafter, Henry started his own graphic design company; where he designed logos, posters, business cards, menus, clothing, C.D. covers and all types of publications. in and around the Jackson, MS area..

Henry moved back to New York City in 2005 and became a teacher. Earning a dual masters degree in education and special education in 2010. Henry later went back to school and earned a third masters degree in instructional technology from Touro College in 2018.

Currently, Henry is married and has one son, and resides in Brooklyn, N.Y. where he teaches 4th grade and enjoys being an author, artist, graphic designer, playwright and songwriter.

OCT   2020
$ 9.99